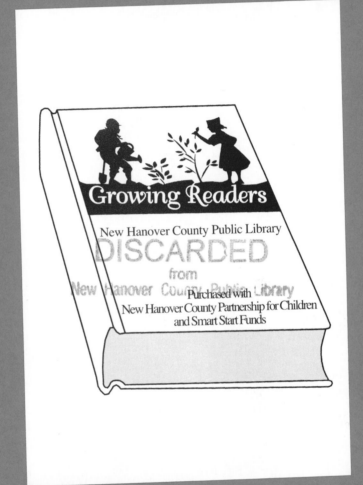

I Love You
Just the Same

Written and illustrated by
Erica Wolf

Henry Holt and Company
New York

Henry Holt and Company, LLC
Publishers since 1866
115 West 18th Street
New York, New York 10011
www.henryholt.com

Library of Congress Cataloging-in-Publication Data
Wolf, Erica.
I love you just the same / Erica Wolf.
Summary: Throughout the year, a little bear struggles to learn the things
his mother teaches, but she reassures him of her love no matter what he does.
[1. Love—Fiction. 2. Mother and child—Fiction. 3. Growth—Fiction. 4. Bears—Fiction.]
I. Title. PZ7.W8185517Is 2003   [E]—dc21   2002012835

ISBN 0-8050-7128-8 / First Edition—2003 / Designed by Donna Mark
Printed in the United States of America on acid-free paper. ∞

1 3 5 7 9 10 8 6 4 2

The artist used acrylics on Rives BFK paper
to create the illustrations for this book.

To my family and Ro-bear
for supporting
my dreams

As the sun came up, Little Bear felt his mother's warm nose nudging him gently.

"Come, Little Bear. Spring has arrived, and it's time for us to leave our den."

Following closely behind his mother, Little Bear
stepped outside and looked around in wonder
at what he saw.

The winter snow had melted, and in its place grew
fresh green grass and bright, delicate flowers.

Little Bear saw his mother munching on the grass and decided to taste it himself. It was crunchy and sweet, but hard to chew.

"That's all right, Little Bear. In time you will have teeth big enough to chew all the grass you can eat. The most important thing is that you tried your best. I still love you just the same."

Soon the days grew longer, as did the grass.
"Come, Little Bear. Summer has arrived, and it's
time for you to learn how to fish."

Little Bear watched patiently while his mother waded into the rushing stream. She stood very still for a few moments and then—*swoosh!*—splashed down into the water. When Mother Bear surfaced she had a big silver fish in her mouth.

Little Bear waded into the shallow water and tried his best to do what his mother had shown him. He stood very still and watched, waiting for a fish to swim by, and then—*swoosh!*—splashed down into the water. But when he came up he had nothing in his mouth.

"That's all right, Little Bear. In time you will be quick enough to catch a fish. The most important thing is that you tried your best. I still love you just the same."

Then the air grew crisp, and the leaves turned golden.

"Come, Little Bear. Fall has arrived, and it's time for you to learn how to dig for roots."

Little Bear watched intently while his mother sniffed the
forest floor and then, using her massive claws, dug deep into
the earth, revealing tender roots and other tasty morsels.

Little Bear tried his best to dig in the ground, but his claws couldn't do much more than scratch the surface.

"That's all right, Little Bear. In time you
will have claws big enough to dig for roots. The
most important thing is that you tried your best.
I still love you just the same."

The trees were soon bare, and the snow began to fall. "Come, Little Bear. Winter is almost here, and it's time for us to return to our den."

As Little Bear and his mother made the long trip back to their den, he thought of all the things she had tried to teach him, but he was sad because he wasn't able to do any of them.

"That's all right, Little Bear. In time you will grow big and be able to do all the things I have shown you. The most important thing is that you tried your best. I still love you just the same."

"Good night, Little Bear. . . . Sleep tight."

After a long winter's nap, cold winds gave way once again to warm spring breezes. This time, however, it was Little Bear who eagerly nudged his mother awake.

"Come, Mother. Spring has arrived, and it's time for us to leave our den."

This year Little Bear could chew
the green grass with ease.

He was quick
enough to catch
silver fish,

and his claws
were big enough
to dig for roots
in the ground.

"I'm so proud of you, Little Bear. And
even though you're not so little anymore,
I still love you just the same."